This Noelle

By

USA TODAY Bestselling Author

KRISTIN HOLT

www.KristinHolt.com

eBook and Paperback Cover designs © 2015 by Teresa Allen.
eBook and Paperback interior design by Kristin Holt.
Editing by RVP The Man Editing:
https://RVPTheManEditing.weebly.com/

Priase for This Noelle

❄

To Kristin.

"I read *This Noelle* last night and I just had to let you know my feelings on the book. First let me say I saw it was available weeks ago and just couldn't read it. Not sure what changed but last night I had some time and decided to take a look at it. I was prepared to hate it but determined not to let it affect how I felt about you as an author. It's impossible to read a book this emotionally charged and not have it change things. This book will play over and over in my head for a long time. It is possibly the best piece of fiction I have ever read. It's potentially easy to bring two people together and let them heal each other. When they have caused each other's pain it's an entirely different ballgame. I am so beyond impressed with how you portrayed Phil as repentant. He never tried to blame her distance for his straying. You never allowed her to play the scorned wife. She was grieving and hurting and dealt as best she could and he was grieving and hurting and dealt as best he could.

When she invited him back to bed just to hold her I cried. When she invited him to resume the physical aspects of their marriage I again cried. When they spent the crazy Christmas 9 years later and were both tired and flustered and they sent all the children for an hour rest I again cried. They found the way to keep anything else from coming between them. I loved the closing line when the kids find their parents bedroom door locked. I laughed out loud and caused my husband to pause what he was doing and ask why I laughed so hard. I read him the scene and he responded with, "I like that author! Did you tell her about ..." well never mind what else he said."

~ Amy P, reader and reviewer

Shared with permission.

Dedication

To my readers, with gratitude.

Thank you for your ongoing and gracious support. Thank you for giving my books a chance, sharing them with your friends and family, and reviewing them on Amazon and Goodreads. *You* make all the difference.

This
Noelle

Dear Reader,

I find it necessary to give a disclaimer before you read a single word.

This book deals with sensitive and tender subjects. I have yet to find a woman (or man) who says, "Yes! Let me read about infidelity! I just *adore* that subject and it leaves me feeling all warm and fuzzy inside."

I'm taking a king-sized risk offering this title as my gift to readers. Some will argue I should offer this one for sale (because readers are choosy and will pass this title by if it's something they're not interested in, and especially if they've lived through the heartrending agony of infidelity) and give away a different story. Maybe a light, fluffy, simple mail-order bride tale about a couple that teases each other and falls in love over coffee and chocolate cake and lives happily ever after without too much difficulty.

I could. And I might. Maybe next year.

But I feel moved to delve into a richer, deeper subject... while remaining consistent with the parameters of Sweet Romance. (Wholesome, innocent, clean.) Even in books without foul language and without sex actively shown, conflict is the stuff books are made of.

No conflict, no story.

My books have shown more and more conflict, the better I understand it. Stronger villains. Issues like U.S. Marshal August Rose faced in *The Marshal's Surrender* (a dangerous gang of miscreants committing offenses a judge would hang them for).

Would Phil Finlay and his wife, Caroline, have really discovered one another— *and fallen in love for keeps*— if not for the crucible of conflict they face in *This Noelle*?

Yes, this book obviously contains (see the book description) the consequences of Phil's infidelity. Where else would the surprise new baby come from? I must emphasize one thing: **this story is *far less* about a cheating husband and *far more* about a husband and wife who fall in love, again.**

Maybe their second chance at love and happiness comes about because, at Christmastime, their hearts are a little softer and their souls a little more open to everything Christmas means to Christians.

Maybe this fictional couple's love story didn't happen *before* marriage... but *after*.

Maybe, just maybe, the miracle of a Newborn King in Bethlehem two millennia hence might heal a brokenhearted mother.

I hope you'll read *This Noelle* with a simple question in your heart: ***What would* I *do?***

My heart is filled with compassion for women like Caroline (the fictional wife and mother in this story). Caroline is grieving the loss of her own son, Peter, but must also make a choice— perhaps one of the most difficult choices a wife and mother must ever make, especially in today's world.

Caroline had fewer choices than you and I. She couldn't get by in 1881, in a frontier town, on a farm, without a man. At least, not easily. Her children are small. She has no grown sons to work the ranch and no money to pay hired laborers. Twenty-first century women can and do support themselves and their families when their marriages dissolve. Today's women might well say, "My man cheats on me, and he's gone. I'd never stay with him. And he knows it."

I respect every woman's choice.

I wouldn't dare tell my mother, sister, daughter, coworker, or friend what she should or shouldn't do, if faced with life-altering news such as Caroline's. What any woman— *then or now*— does upon hearing what happened between her husband and the ever-detested "other woman" (and might I also suggest when men hear about their wife and the ever-detested "other man") is as unique, personal, and singular as the individual's fingerprint.

What would you do?

How would you know what you'd do, until you lived it?

Until you weighed the offenses against your spouse's attitude?

Until you looked your partner in the eye, Christmas or not, and asked, "Where do we go from here?"

How would a helpless, innocent newborn— and the desperate craving of your heart— change things?

If your spouse were penitent, apologetic, desperate for forgiveness, would that sway you?

What *if*?

Kristin

Chapter One

Saturday, December 24, 1881
Mountain Home, Colorado

Phil Finlay's comeuppance arrived on the steps of the community church.

One glance at young Jasper Jones riding into the churchyard, squalling baby tucked into the crook of an arm, and Phil *knew*.

Still, he counted backward, December to March. *Nine months*.

His broken heart rattled loose and tumbled,

clear to his boots.

He'd made plenty of mistakes in his life—and some evoked far more shame and regret than others. *This* happened to be the granddaddy of 'em all.

At his back, behind the closed double doors, the brand-new church organ pumped the opening measures of *O Holy Night*.

If he'd thought, for one moment, his wife was strong enough to hear his confession, he'd would've come clean long ago.

Caroline had been so frail then a stiff breeze could've knocked her off her feet. She wasn't any better prepared tonight than she'd been yesterday or last week or *months* ago.

He swallowed with the raw, agonizing pain that had been a constant companion since Peter's Day.

Some losses never faded, not a speck.

Nearly eleven months later, he didn't know if it ever would.

He had to face the music, though he still had no idea how to prevent this from destroying his wife.

His growing headache throbbed in time with his broken heart.

He drew a deep breath, and the cold burned his lungs.

The strains of piano and voice swelled. *It is the night of our dear Savior's birth...*

Young Jasper had obviously caught sight of

Phil on the church steps because he wheeled his spotted pony between parked sleighs. The babe's cries grew louder, above the Christmas hymn.

A furtive glance about the darkening churchyard, and Phil noted others still making their way inside. Doc Cheney set his brake, hopped down from his two-seater, and made his way around to assist his young bride.

Shame boiled over.

Phil didn't want an audience. But it couldn't be helped. If he turned tail and ran into the church, dodging the inevitable, the boy would no doubt follow him inside.

No.

He'd done what he'd done, and he'd own up to the consequences.

Jasper pulled his pony to a halt, right beside the church steps. At the cusp of adolescence, the boy was all elbows and knees, with hands and nose and feet too big for the rest of him.

The blacksmith and his bride thumped up the steps, nodding in greeting, and bustled inside. The open doorway amplified the organ music and congregation singing and a wash of warm air. Candlelight from within splashed over the steps, illuminating Jasper's stark misery. Too much to bear. The boy's coat sleeves were far too short on his rapidly growing frame.

...Long lay the world in sin and error pining, till He appeared...

Doc and Mrs. Cheney paused on the steps.

"Your ma delivered? How's she getting on?"

Jasper lifted a thin shoulder, his attention on the reins clasped in a chapped fist. "Died couple hours ago, birthin' this girl."

One more sin heaped upon the others. *A woman's life.*

Dear God!

...Fall on your knees, O hear the angel voices!....

Mrs. Cheney gasped.

"Here, let me take the baby." Doc reached for the bawling infant.

Her tiny fist waved free of her wrappings.

Dimly, through the numbness that had stolen his voice, Phil dragged his gaze from the babe to Jasper's face.

...O Night Divine...

"Nah, Doc." Jasper pushed the baby on Phil.

With numb, trembling hands, he accepted the babe, compassion for the little one's distress overriding everything else. So small, barely six pounds, he'd guess. He wrapped the single quilt about the tiny body.

No one had bathed her. Fluids from the birthing had dried on the babe's skin and matted dark hair. Her cries waned as he snuggled her close.

...Truly He taught us to love one another...

"A'fore Ma died, she told me to take this 'un to you," Jasper said, his youthful voice strangled with pain, "said *you're* her pa."

On Christmas Eve, Caroline sat in church with five small children.

She'd bundled up the little ones against the cold and come to town because church had seemed the right thing to do. And because she *needed* peace.

If only she could feel the joy in the season she once had.

If only she could *feel*.

Sprigs of evergreen decorated the ends of the pews, tied with red velvet bows. Candles glowed from every sconce and candelabra. Mrs. Gilbert, at the organ, played the closing chords of *O Holy Night*.

Pastor Gilbert claimed the podium, preparing to impart a prayer just as Phil approached the end of their pew. His boot heels dragged on the plank floor. Caroline shushed Del, Harold, Luke, Miranda, and Mary Beth, then slid in a few more inches to make room.

Why didn't Phil sit? He wasn't one to dawdle with the sleigh and team or make the preacher wait. The congregation had fallen silent, most awaiting the opening words of the prayer. Caroline clasped her hands and bowed her head.

The preacher prayed, and Phil lowered himself into the space beside her. His big, solid, warm body pressed against her side.

Before Pastor Gilbert made it halfway through his prayer of thanksgiving, Phil leaned near and passed a squirming bundle into her hands. Like so many times before, as if by rote, she took a babe from his grasp and the great void in her heart yawned wider than ever.

Immediate tears stung her eyes and burned at the back of her throat. What a cruel gesture, this forcing of a babe into arms that still ached to cradle her lost son.

Whose infant was this?

She'd barely glanced at the babe's tiny, wrinkled face, her broken heart bleeding at the cruelty in his gesture. What made him think she wanted to hold a baby?

And *who*, pray tell, would bring out a *newborn* in winter?

True, she hadn't been as social in the past year since Peter had been born and lived his short life. He had entered and exited this world in the space of a single day. Her heart, despite his elder brothers and sisters needing care and a mother's love, hadn't begun to heal. She'd not held a single infant since Peter.

Most of the women about Mountain Home understood her reticence.

Apparently, her husband did not.

Phil clasped his large, work-roughened hands between his knees, apparently caught up in prayer. His lips moved silently as if petitioning God, even while the pastor prayed aloud.

Did he pray for *her?* For a Christmas miracle to heal her heart of the tragic loss of their infant son? She'd never seen him pray with such focus and intent... unless it was for her.

Phil's fervency *should* touch her. It *should.*

Why couldn't she *feel?*

The unknown babe in her hands fussed, squirmed, and crinkled its features in misery. For the first time, her gaze focused on the little one's face, noted the dried blood and fluids— evidenced by creamy white residue on his skin and wrinkled, tiny fingers— sure signs he couldn't be more than a few hours old and hadn't been properly bathed.

The babe's quilt had seen much use and many washings. Inadequate to keep a newborn warm in weather like this. Who would bring a babe out among so many souls improperly wrapped? Did its mother have no common sense? The child could catch its death of cold.

She wrapped the little one more snugly, and even as the congregation murmured their amens to the prayer, she'd tucked the baby against the warmth of her body and pulled her cloak about them both.

No matter whose child this was, no matter

what Phil had been thinking when he'd put this little one in her arms, she was a mother first and foremost and could not allow this baby to suffer.

The choir rose. Plump and dowdy Mrs. Barnes stood with her back to the congregation, marking time with her baton and signaled the tenors' opening notes.

Anyone could see this babe needed a good feeding. The nappy was wet all the way through, and he'd lose more body heat if not changed. Behind them, a man sneezed, murmured "pardon me," and blew his nose into a hanky.

No place for a newborn.

A winter birth. Like Peter's. The painful memories sliced through her broken heart like a boot heel on crushed glass. Too much. Far too much. If she knew whose child this was, she'd return it forthwith, pray the mother had wits enough to safeguard her child, and—

She met her husband's gaze and read poignant sadness and regret in his deep blue eyes. He couldn't mask the discomfort and something far worse— *panic?*— as his gaze slid from hers to the infant in her arms. The little mouth opened in a wide yawn, and something inside Caroline's frozen heart eased... just a little.

It seemed so very unlikely, so unfathomable that cradling a borrowed infant while the choir sang a familiar Christmas melody could bring warmth into her heart, frozen over these past ten months. She adjusted the edge of her cape over the babe's brow so only his little eyes and nose were exposed.

The choir had finished their number so she couldn't whisper without drawing attention. "Whose child is this?" she mouthed.

He blinked and held her gaze. He swallowed, his Adam's apple bobbing in his lean throat.

He surprised her by slipping an arm about her shoulders, snuggling her against his side— odd, as he'd gradually stopped touching her altogether. He seemed to anchor her in place with that contact, grounding her.

His touch felt both wonderful and terrible, panic she didn't understand flared sharp and vivid. In the quiet of the church, the minister paused in his address and cleared his throat. He might be waiting for Phil and Caroline to return their attention to his message. But, in that moment, she couldn't care about his words about the birth of the Holy Child.

She must know about *this* child. Why would her husband push someone else's newborn on her in church?

Phil leaned near, his lips brushing her ear. The warmth of his breath, at once so familiar and comforting also brought a surge of dread. She knew her husband so well, knew him through and through. The man trembled in his boots.

Something about the shape of the babe's newborn eyes— and chin?— evoked strong recollections of six little ones. Del. Harold. Luke. Miranda. Mary Beth. *Peter*.

Something was amiss. Very wrong.

"Whose...?" Her throat constricted, closing over the question she could not ask.

The fine hairs at her nape stood on end, and she closed her eyes against the stark resemblance between the babe in her arms and her own six children.

She swallowed, hard. "Whose child?"

It seemed imprudent to ask for she feared she already knew the truth.

"Mine," Phil whispered. "This baby is mine."

Chapter Two

March 1881
Nine months ago...

Climbing onto the Jones's cabin roof had been easy.

Sliding off onto the eave-high drifts, even easier.

In Phil's entire life— first New England, then Pennsylvania, and finally, the Colorado Rockies— he'd *never* seen a winter like this.

The end of March, and the spring thaw was

nowhere in sight. Some folks prayed incessantly, sure God extracted vengeance for some sin or another.

Phil was of the mindset that this was one of those freak winters like the one back in '16. The year without a summer. Old folks still talked about that year-long winter.

This long winter would end, eventually. But if he didn't clear the poorly built roof of snow and shore it up, Widow Jones's cabin wouldn't survive beneath the weight.

"Jasper!" Phil spun about, looking for the kid. He'd disappeared, leaving Phil alone to shovel off the roof.

The boy's dishwater-blond head popped up over the edge of the eaves. "Took you twenty shovels to notice me gone this time."

Phil wiped the sweat off his brow. The physical exertion felt good.

As did helping the widow and her children.

When the citizens of Mountain Home had met to discuss the list of emergency needs, the mayor had passed the job of repairing Widow Jones's roof to Phil, a master carpenter. If anyone could remake a standing cabin and ensure it stood 'til winter finally broke, that somebody was Phil.

He'd been glad to help.

Truth be told, he'd *needed* to be needed.

He hadn't known how badly he'd needed conversation, companionship, friendly company, until he'd begun the two days' work. The first had passed quickly and easily.

Leaving behind the silence of his home, a wife who looked through him, spoke rarely and only to the children, had been...

Wonderful?

A relief?

A guilty pleasure?

Here, he could push aside his own crushing secrets and haunting memories. The nightmares wouldn't stop— so he'd taken to sleeping on the parlor floor as to not wake Caroline.

He'd barely thought of Peter or death or those memories while clearing snow that day. As he enjoyed a steaming bowl of venison stew at Widow Jones's table, he realized he'd only thought of Peter once. "Thank you, ma'am."

"Thank you, Mr. Finlay, for your fine work." She wasn't a handsome woman, some five— maybe ten?— years his senior.

Until she smiled.

Odd, wasn't it? How a smile could lend handsomeness to otherwise plain features.

The conversation that had begun with the weather had morphed, much like her, from plain and everyday to something remarkable. Mrs. Jones had plenty to say.

She laughed. She listened. She asked questions.

And her pale eyes sparkled with interest in all he said.

He enjoyed more conversation, more companionship at the Jones's table than he'd known at home in a month of Sundays.

He didn't mean to compare, didn't *want* to compare. Honest, he didn't.

Things hadn't been good at home for a long while. First, the children had come so close together, sapping Caroline's strength and taxing her patience. Then Peter.

He drew in a deep breath, shaking off the painful memories. The storm that night, in white-out conditions, had made going for Doc Cheney nearly impossible. Only to find the Doc and his wife had been called out and pinned down by the storm.

He'd been forced to deliver Peter himself.

"You're worried," Emma Jones noted. "You don't think you can strengthen the roof?"

"Not at all. Just tired."

"Oh?"

"Now that the snow is cleared, I'll spend tomorrow shoring up the roof and patching the leaking spots. Should finish up by dusk tomorrow."

"You think the mayor might add a snowball skirmish to Founders' Day?"

"In August?" He couldn't help but laugh. Laughing felt so blessedly good. "That'd be a sight to behold."

"Wouldn't it, though?" Her hair, not blonde, not brown by gray afternoon sunlight had burnished golden by lamplight. "I expect winter won't relinquish its hold until June. Everybody's ice houses will be full, still, into July and August. I fancy ice cream at Founder's Day."

"Mmm. That sounds delicious." Though now, the hot food warmed him from the inside out. The venison stew was hardy, flavorful, and stuck to his ribs.

They lingered at the table over coffee and simple spice cookies. Eventually, her daughter asked to be excused and washed the dishes without being asked. More time lapsed as talk of the incomparable winter storms that kept the trains from running gave way to speculations about when supplies would finally make their way through.

Widow Jones touched Phil's shoulder. A simple, kind, gentle touch— a human touch.

A thrill shot through him, though surely she didn't mean anything by it.

She shouldn't touch him, even in friendship. And *he*, well, he shouldn't respond with the urgency to pull her close.

A most unmanly rush of emotion surged to the surface. Grief and loss, knotted up in loneliness so acute he couldn't bear it. He craved her touch, *needed* her touch.

Her pale eyes held his for long, long moments. He had the most disconcerting awareness that this woman he barely knew saw through the superficial to the man beneath.

A man who didn't deserve a crumb of kindness.

"Jasper." Emma Jones's focus upon Phil's face never wavered. "Go on now. See to the evening chores."

"Yes, Ma."

The boy bundled up and eventually the door shut behind her son, and still, her eyes caressed Phil.

He should go. Strap on his snowshoes and head for home.

Barring another whiteout, he'd make it back to the ranch within three hours.

He'd be fine. He'd only spent the entire workday outside in the cold. What was another three hours?

Emma's fingertip traced the seam on his jacket's shoulder.

He shouldn't feel a thing. She exerted no pressure. None at all.

Yet he sensed her touch through numerous layers of clothing.

And her touch stirred frightening needs to life.

He should *go*. Now.

Leave the tools he'd just dried and oiled. Leave them behind.

Flee temptation.

He swallowed, hard. "Mrs. Jones—"

"Emma. My name is Emma." The stroke of her finger along his jaw, life-giving rain to parched, drought-battered soil.

When she slipped her work-roughened hand into his, he didn't resist.

He felt like a dog beneath the table, begging for scraps. And starving, never getting enough to eat.

Her smile softened as she stood.

He paused, banishing all thought.

Until she tugged on his hand. So warm, sincere, solid. Filled with kindness.

Kindness he certainly didn't deserve.

How long had it been since his wife had touched him?

No.

No.

Don't think.

Mrs. Jones, Emma, opened her bedroom door, Phil's hand still tight in hers.

An invitation danced in the sparkle of her eyes, unspoken, at least with words. But the invitation was made, just the same.

Grief and pain welled within him, swelling and chafing until he doubted he'd control the unwanted emotions.

Emma tipped up her face to search Phil's eyes.

What would she see there?

Grief? Hesitancy? Pain?

Don't think.

Emma laced her fingers between his. So warm. So solid. So certain.

She entered her bedroom, and Phil followed.

Chapter Three

Caroline couldn't stand the press of bodies, the closeness of the warmed air in the church. Christmas Eve or not, she couldn't bear to remain one moment longer.

Desperation to escape the confines of the building clamped its fist about her throat.

Air. She needed air.

She pushed past Phil. He didn't try to stop her.

As she fled up the aisle to the doors, it seemed every eye was on her. Friends.

Neighbors. Acquaintances. Their faces reflecting questions and concern and curiosity.

Before she reached the door, she heard Phil close on her heels. A quick glance over her shoulder— Phil had Miranda on one arm and Mary Beth on the other. Three little boys trailed behind.

She fumbled with the doorknob, pushed the heavy door open, and immediately slipped on the icy stoop.

She clung to the infant in her arms even as her boots skated out from beneath her. She landed hard upon her backside, pain jolting up her spine and would have clacked her teeth together if she'd not already clenched her jaw.

The babe startled and wailed in an unmistakable newborn's cry.

The *child*.

By some miracle, she'd protected the babe— the little thing wasn't harmed.

No one should trust her with a baby. Not now. Maybe not ever.

Phil must've shut the church's door, and set their children upon their feet, for he scooped Caroline up almost instantly. His breath showed in a cloud of frosted white in the night air.

She couldn't see his features clearly in the wan light spilling from stained glass windows, nor glowing in lanterns hanging from sleighs.

"Are you all right?" Phil clutched her elbows tighter, steadying her.

All right? No, she wasn't all right. She'd *never* be all right.

Already, winter's cold had seeped through her cape, her woolen dress and stockings, numerous petticoats. Numb. She was so ridiculously numb.

Numb to the pain anyone else would feel from a fall upon icy steps.

Numb to the stares of the congregation as she fled Christmas Eve candlelight service.

Numb to her husband's perfidy.

"Bring the children," she ordered Phil. "We are leaving."

Without fear, without caution, she hurried down the stairs and across the snowy yard to their sleigh.

Behind her, Miranda, too little to understand, wailed.

Phil hushed her and hurried to keep up.

Caroline climbed into the sleigh, refusing help. Instead, Phil settled the little ones in the space behind the seat, wrapped them in quilts and talked softly to soothe them.

The babe in her arms stretched, arched its little back, and cried piteously.

What was she to *do*?

Think! Think—

Her thoughts were as muddled, thick as mud— just as they'd been on that fateful day in early February.

Phil settled himself on the seat, flicked the

reins, and the sleigh lurched into motion. Bells jingled. The newborn's cries tore at whatever meager healing she'd managed in the past year.

What *now*?

She couldn't mother this child. Not *this* child.

Something had frozen solid within her the past winter with Peter's death. She'd not *felt*— not anything— since.

She barely kept her five children fed, clean, and cared for.

What was she to do with a newborn?

The babe wailed harder. Against her will, Caroline snuggled the little body closer, ensuring her cape adequately covered everything but the little one's mouth and nose. She found herself rocking side to side and smoothing a hand over the infant's back.

Someone had to take care of this babe. *Someone* must.

Phil drove the team beside her, his body tense. Did she know this man, her husband?

"Who," she demanded, watching his profile, illuminated sharply by sleigh lanterns, "is this child's mother?"

A sound of anguish twisted from his throat. "Mrs. Jones."

Who?

Why didn't the identity of the woman evoke fury? Why did Caroline still feel trapped beneath eight inches of ice?

Mrs. Jones... *Mrs. Jones...* A widow woman with half-grown children, whose spread lay on the north side of Mountain Home. She'd kept to herself, mostly, since her husband had died in a mining cave-in a few years back. The Joneses weren't the kind to appreciate organized religion. Caroline thought she'd recognize the woman... maybe. Had they *ever* exchanged words?

How did Phil know Widow Jones?

She tried to summon the anger she should feel, the fury she wanted, *needed*.

What Christian woman would accept this news without reacting?

She should react, say something. "Mrs. Jones brought this child to church— why? Hasn't she the sense to keep a newborn at home?"

Try as she might, Caroline couldn't summon more than an apathetic, mild aggravation for the widow...

...though she'd borne Caroline's husband a child.

A woman really ought to muster anger over that breach of trust.

"She died." Phil shifted on the seat, rocking as if in physical pain. "She died. In childbirth."

Caroline breathed, waited, felt the life and vitality of the little one in her arms. Why couldn't she feel compassion for this child, whose mother lay dead?

She wanted to feel fury coursing through her veins, self-righteous anger a bellows to that fire of indignation. She wanted to rant and scream and demand answers.

"How do you know?" The calm question was the best she could manage.

"Jasper rode in." He swallowed, his throat clicking with the effort. "Handed her to me on the steps. Said his ma died in the birthing."

So, there was no possibility of giving the child back.

At least, not to its— her?— mother. Phil had said *her*.

Someone would take in the child. Someone gathered at the church for candlelight Christmas Eve services.

The babe rooted at Caroline's breast and a ghost of sensation, as if her milk let down, tingled through her.

The first honest, real sensation, coupled with the first honest emotion in *months*.

Phil had halted the sleigh at the crossroads. Ahead, one of the bays tossed its head.

He awaited instructions.

"Take me home." She tightened her hold around the tiny, helpless child. "Take us home quickly."

An hour later, once the team was cared for, and the little boys and girls were fed and tucked into bed for the night, Phil found Caroline working near the heat of the stove.

His wife hummed softly to his newborn daughter, bathing her in a basin. His aching heart lodged in his throat, making it nearly impossible to draw breath. How many times had he seen his wife care for their children, often long into the night, ministering to them with gentleness and motherly love?

He remembered how things used to be.

Before.

He recalled loving his wife, loving her more than he'd thought a man could love a woman. They'd had a good marriage, then, hadn't they?

His conscience twisted.

When had he stopped loving her? Surely not all at once. No married man ever decided, one day, to cease loving the woman he'd wed and promised his future.

His betrayal would kill whatever remained of her love for him. He knew her so well after their years together. She couldn't love him. Not after this.

Maybe that was for the best. Their marriage had been strained to the breaking point since Peter's death... or perhaps before. He couldn't put a finger on the day things had changed for the worse between them, but change they had.

Even without the appearance of this child,

he and Caroline had been merely pretending for what felt like ages.

If she wanted him to go, he'd go. But who would look after his family? Who would protect them? This high Rocky Mountain valley was no place for a woman alone with young ones.

Maybe she'd let him stay.

Sleeping in the barn wouldn't be so different than sleeping on the parlor floor.

Probably, come spring, she'd want to return to her parents in Pennsylvania.

She must've sensed him in the doorway, for she ceased humming. She finished dressing the babe in soft flannel gowns their children had worn, swaddled her tight, and settled at the table where goat's milk cooled. Without acknowledging his presence, Caroline balanced the little one on the seam of her legs, folded a clean hankie to serve as a teat, and dipped it into the milk. She tested the temperature, and apparently finding it adequately cool, nudged the babe's lips.

His daughter— *his daughter*— squalled, sought the sodden fabric, and finally accepted Caroline's care. When the babe had sucked the fabric dry, she moved the little one into the crook of her elbow and refilled the fabric with milk.

His wife made soothing sounds. Sweet, motherly noises he remembered from the countless times she'd nursed their babies. Pain, acute, poignant, sharp.

How had he ever stopped loving her?

Those memories resurfaced, threatened to make everything worse. Now was not the time to let tender emotions run amok. Their marriage was ending, not beginning. He'd be a fool to let himself remember all that had once been.

Another dip of cotton into milk, and more greedy gulping from a baby girl with a tuft of dark hair upon her crown. In the golden lamplight, the little one's satin skin and downy hair reminded him so much of Peter in those few precious hours.

How had he allowed his grief to steal more from him? From *them?*

Hadn't Caroline already lost enough? Hadn't he?

Hadn't Emma Jones?

He'd ruined *everything.*

"I'm sorry." The blurted confession sounded hoarse, pathetic.

And he was. Desperately sorry. For all they'd had and all they'd lost.

Caroline set the hankie upon a clean plate beside the pan of milk and lifted the babe to her shoulder. As she rubbed and patted his daughter's little back, she slowly lifted her gaze to his. "How do you know this baby is yours?"

The question caught him off guard. "Jasper said..." Jasper had delivered his mother's dying message. *A'fore Ma died, she told me to take this 'un to you, said* you're *her pa.*

"Jasper is Widow Jones's son?"

He nodded, not sure where Caroline was headed with this. Her calm tone angered him. If only she'd accuse him, fight back, raise her voice— he'd at least know she cared.

She patted the infant's back and urged a burp. She continued rubbing in gentle circles. "I'll ask again. How do you *know* this child is yours?"

Stunned, he considered her question. A serious question. An important question.

All he knew for sure was that the timing was right. He *could have* fathered this child.

Maybe Jasper had a bone to pick— and decided to hurt Phil and his family by presenting a baby someone else had actually fathered. Another man could have been keeping company with Widow Jones.

Maybe the girl wasn't even his mother's. For all they knew, Emma was alive and well and hadn't given birth.

Grasping at straws. Looking for a way out. Telling stories. It didn't suit.

He watched his wife snuggle his apparent daughter to her breast and offer more warmed milk on the hankie.

"I ought to make sure this infant doesn't belong to a living woman who wants her back."

"I agree."

"With your permission, I'll ride out there at first light. If Widow Jones did die in childbed, someone ought to make sure her children have a place to go." That someone might as well be him.

"Of course."

The Caroline he'd loved and married seven years earlier wouldn't have taken this news without a fight. Seeing her like this— cold, aloof, uninterested, a mere shadow of the woman she'd once been— broke his heart.

If *this* didn't garner her attention, what would?

"What if," he asked, watching carefully for any hint of emotional connection. "What if Jasper's tale is true? What if this child is motherless?"

His wife remained silent for several long moments. She finally glanced at him for the briefest of seconds— just long enough for him to glimpse pain in her eyes. "I don't know."

Chapter Four

The following morning, Caroline had barely succeeded in shooing Phil, dressed for travel and well-fed, out of the house when the unwelcome jingle of sleigh bells announced an arrival.

Visitors, at this hour?

Snuggling the fussing baby closer, she lifted the curtain to peer through the frosted windowpane. Sure enough, their young minister, with his even younger bride, had just halted his team in her dooryard.

Caroline fought the urge to scream.

Phil *needed* to go. Through the long hours of the night, she'd thought about those other children. Jasper and his sister. Did they have anyone, now, when desperately needed? From painful experience, she knew that grave-digging, beneath winter's snowfall, took a grown man hours. Jasper, not yet a man, *needed* help. Whether he'd accept help from Phil remained to be seen.

She watched Phil greet the minister. The low rumble of voices carried through the stout cabin walls, but not their words. Phil's posture said it all.

The children scampered from their bedroom to the main room and back again, their laughter and happiness a stark contrast to her misery.

"Del," she told her eldest, "take your brothers and sisters into the bedroom. Play with your blocks."

If Del heard, he didn't acknowledge.

She quickly followed. "Papa has a visitor. It's time to play quietly."

Miranda upended the flour sack containing blocks onto the rag rug. She shook the sack and two more tumbled free. Dropping to his knees, Luke grabbed the gaily painted green and red blocks.

A quick pause to wrap the infant more snuggly in a quilt, and Caroline met the visitors and Phil in the main room. A rush of frigid air and the crisp scent of pine and lingering wood smoke had swept through the open door.

"Merry Christmas to you!" Gilbert stomped the snow off his boots and removed his hat.

Caroline smothered a wince— it was Christmas morning, wasn't it?

Phil took their coats, invited the Gilberts to sit, and unwrapped himself.

Caroline forced a smile she couldn't feel and offered hot drinks.

When at last they settled near the hearth, the pastor set his cup on the saucer and with surprising calm and no hint of embarrassment asked, "We've come to see how we might be of help to your family."

He searched Caroline's face until discomfort drove her attention to her husband. Phil had the good sense to speak for them. "You wonder about the baby."

She might revere Pastor Gilbert's calling, but take counsel from a man barely old enough to shave? The baby continued fussing, so she stood to jostle her gently.

"Indeed I do. Obviously, if this little one were yours, you'd have carried him into the church with the other children, not left him outside with his papa, while he saw to the horses."

He was right, of course. Caroline couldn't meet the preacher's eye.

Gilbert sounded anything but judgmental.

"The poor thing seemed a castoff. When you brought it in from the cold, Phil, I had to wonder if you'd found a squalling bundle on the church steps."

Phil gripped the back of his neck and massaged as if a headache troubled him. He let his breath go in a whoosh. "Something like that."

"If the infant boy was left on the steps of my church, I feel obligated to see he's cared for."

"She." Caroline surprised herself. Moments ago, she'd been content to let Phil handle this. "The baby is a girl."

"Very well, a girl. I expect we'll find someone willing to adopt her."

Give her away?

A twinge of something... uncomfortable... itched at the thought of sending the baby to adoptive parents.

During the long winter's night, Caroline had become quite attached to the little mite. A bit selfish... Yet, until Phil went on his errand to the Jones place, the girl wasn't theirs to give up, now was she?

The young preacher turned to Phil. "Several people were still entering the church, so the foundling couldn't have been on the step more than a minute. Did you see who left her there?"

Foundling implied a birth in shame, a child a mother couldn't keep because she was unwed.

Hadn't she witnessed the consequences of illegitimacy, just a couple years ago, when

Temperance Cartwright's half-sister appeared in Mountain Home? Felicity's life had been plagued by the judgmental, from her birth. She'd suffered consequences into adulthood.

How could Caroline allow that to happen? To *any* child? Much less one *probably* sharing blood with her own babies, strongly resembled them, and bore no fault?

How could Caroline consign Phil's daughter to a life ruined by illegitimacy?

They didn't know for sure if the babe was Phil's issue... But in her heart, Caroline *knew*.

She saw every one of her babies in the infant girl's face, in the curl of her perfectly formed ears, the shape of her pink lips.

The precious child was *innocent,* no matter which side of the blanket she'd been born on. She deserved a family, protection, a home. She deserved the Finlay name. She deserved love and affection and a place to belong. Here, she had brothers and sisters. She had a father. *And* a mother.

Caroline sucked in a breath, stunned. She *wanted* this baby.

This baby.

This reminder.

It made no sense, had no justification. *Why* wasn't she jumping at the opportunity to rid herself of an infant whose very existence proved her husband's unfaithfulness?

What woman would tolerate such a

reminder in her home?

The Reverend Gilbert was still talking. She'd missed something, but grasped onto the conversation as he pressed forward. "...give her a good home. We'll see she's raised in the light of the Gospel of Jesus Christ."

Out of nowhere, grief— hot and sharp— lanced through her breast.

Emotion. Unwelcome, overwhelming, enormous in its scope.

She *felt* something.

And it *hurt*.

"Oh, Mrs. Finlay, do forgive me." Pastor Gilbert looked about for a place to set his teacup. "I see your pain, your tears, and fear I've overstepped by bounds."

Tears? Caroline touched her cheeks, stunned to find wetness there.

Tears.

She'd not wept since Peter's Day.

"It must be difficult to have a babe in your home, all of a sudden and without notice. I know the loss of your son was devastating."

If only he knew the whole of it.

Caroline blotted tears with her hankie but managed to nod in acceptance of the minister's words. Emotion thickened her throat, made speech impossible. The ice in her soul was cracking.

To make matters worse, Phil watched her closely, then finally cleared his throat— a sure sign of nervousness. *"Foundling."* His quick glance confirmed he found the term unacceptable and intended to take responsibility. "Yes. I know who put this baby in my arms."

Her heart pounded. What would he say?

Phil drew a shaky breath. His pain and anxiety over confessing all were apparent. No doubt the Gilberts recognized it too.

Seconds ticked by on the clock upon the mantel. In the bedroom, Luke wailed and the tumble of blocks rolling from the carpet to the floorboards.

"I assure you, anything you tell Mrs. Gilbert and me will be held in the highest confidence. I feel called of the Lord to minister in this time of need. I couldn't sleep last night, so great was the urgency to come to you."

"Please," Mrs. Gilbert echoed, "Let us help."

What could this young, childless couple comprehend about this mess?

She let a long moment slip past, slower than honey poured in December. She read nothing but sincerity on the other couple's faces. Unbidden, her gaze slipped to her husband.

"You know Widow Jones?" Phil leaned forward, resting elbows on his knees. "Jasper Jones moved his family here in the summer of '75, bought the old Campbell homestead."

"Reckon I do." The preacher took a sip then nodded for Phil to continue. "I met the widow and her children last spring, 'bout planting time."

"So you know Jasper died a couple years back, when that mine shaft collapsed. His boy, also called Jasper, and a younger daughter— can't think of her name... Tina? Whatever her name might be, they must be fourteen and twelve by now."

"Fine young people. I invited them to worship with us, but the widow assured me they liked things as they were."

"Young Jasper rode into the churchyard with that baby in tow, said his ma," Phil seemed to choke on his words. He rolled his shoulders. "Said his ma died."

Mrs. Gilbert pressed two fingers to her lips, pain marring her youthful features.

"A tragedy." The preacher shook his head. "Those poor orphaned children."

Panic tore at the cracking ice, making headway in destroying Caroline's every protection. She hugged the little warm body close, fighting the resurgence of memories. Peter, fading. Peter growing cold in her arms.

"I was on my way to see after the Jones family when you arrived."

"It's good of you— well and beyond your Christian duty. But—" The preacher's inexperience showed in the color rising in his cheeks and his inability to hold Phil's gaze directly. "Did Jasper have a message when he asked you to bring the babe in? Did he leave word?"

"Yes sir." Phil's chest expanded with a deep breath. "Jasper left word. Not for you, preacher, and not for our congregation. For me." Again, he scrubbed his hand over the muscles of his neck.

Caroline knew her husband well enough to recognize embarrassment, distress, and shame. It all showed in the bunch of his shoulders, the set of his jaw, the pink tinge to his cheekbones and ears.

"I don't understand."

"What I'm about to say, Pastor, I'm asking you— and Mrs. Gilbert— to keep to yourselves. Will you do that?" Phil's voice dropped, both in volume and register. Pain scraped his tone raw.

"Always." The pastor squeezed his wife's gloved hand.

Mrs. Gilbert nodded and glanced from Caroline to Phil. "Anything you say is for our ears alone."

Phil nodded, apparently accepting their word. "I'll give you the truth. I'm ashamed. It's possible— *probable*— that baby girl is mine."

Caroline expected he'd avert his gaze, but he held the preacher's gaze without flinching. She couldn't help but respect Phil for that.

To their credit, neither Pastor nor Mrs. Gilbert flinched. Almost as if they'd not heard Phil's confession.

"I won't deny my guilt." Phil turned to her then, his blue eyes wet with tears he wouldn't allow to spill. "I did wrong. I beg your forgiveness, Caroline."

Chapter Five

Some idiot, somewhere, had proclaimed confession good for the soul.

Phil had certainly heard that phrase plenty.

Ha! Phil knew otherwise. Confessing hadn't relieved the crushing weight on his chest. Not one iota.

Caroline had yet to respond to his plea. Not one word. No gesture signifying an ounce of hope, the slimmest possibility that maybe, one day, she *might* forgive him.

Her tears had surprised him. And given him

a sliver of hope.

Maybe she still cared about him. Just a speck.

Look at me, he begged.

"Let's go get you saddled up," the preacher suggested, communicating wordlessly with his wife to stay with Caroline, "so you might be on your way."

Phil continued to plead, albeit silently, with Caroline.

As usual, he got a double-helping of indifference. She worried the edge of the quilt and stroked the baby's cheek.

A lump the size of his fist lodged in Phil's throat. He nodded, slipped back into his coat, slammed his hat onto his head, and led the way to the barn. Cold sliced through his heavy coat, but the chill didn't hurt near as bad as his wife's apathy.

What had he expected?

Once inside the dusky shadows, he braced two arms against a stall and hung his head. Some man he'd proved to be.

Weak, prone to temptation, sinful. Why the preacher hadn't bundled up his wife and left straight away, he couldn't understand. Who'd want to associate with the likes of him?

Pastor Gilbert slid the barn door closed, robbing the interior of weak morning light. His boots scuffed over the dirt floor, approaching from behind.

Here it came.

Either a lecture 'bout the fires of hell or a man's responsibilities. He doubted the preacher would condone his behavior. The young buck hadn't ever had a stray thought 'bout a woman. He and the missus were so in love, it hurt to look at them. Made Phil want what was dead and buried.

Phil shuffled the loose straw beneath his boots. He ought to saddle up, but knew the preacher hadn't suggested they come out here to get him on his way. Not yet.

He turned to face the preacher and squared his shoulders. "Speak your mind."

"Do you love your wife?"

What kind of a question was that? "Of course I do."

Pastor Gilbert wasn't buying Phil's emphatic response.

"You loved her when you married. Am I right?"

"Yes." What did this have to do with today?

"Would you say you love her more than your wedding day? Or less?"

Less. A whole lot less.

Didn't *that* emasculate him, show him how far he'd fallen?

Why was this shortcoming hard to admit? Married people fell in and out of love all the time. This was normal. It had to be.

"You know we lost a son, nigh onto a year

ago. That loss changed things.

The preacher nodded, but not without sympathy. "That loss affects your love for your wife, how?"

"I love her fine," he insisted, knowing the lie rang false. "*She* doesn't love *me*. Did you see how she wouldn't so much as look at me when we left the house?"

"I saw."

Phil figured the minister had seen plenty. Too much. Including the fact Phil was headed back to the Jones place— while the permanent consequence of his last visit lay cuddled in Caroline's arms.

Might as well string him up, gut him like a deer, and bleed him dry. *Eviscerated*— that word fit precisely. Phil had been eviscerated.

By his wife's indifference.

By his own abominable choices.

By the chain of falling dominoes that led him to this lowest pit in his life. A pit he couldn't see a way out of.

He *couldn't* make things right. No matter what he did, he couldn't turn back time and undo what he'd done.

Not to save Peter's life, not to send somebody else to repair the Jones roof, and not to salvage his wife's love.

Though why he ever expected her to love him in the first place, he couldn't say.

He'd failed Caroline on three counts.

No undoing that.

He'd not slept a wink overnight, for the crushing weight of that realization. He'd taken up his pallet on the parlor floor, where he'd slept since he'd taken ill the week before Peter's short life. Somehow, he'd never made his way back into their bed.

Now that seemed for the best.

So why did it hurt, sure as a knife to his guts?

"You and Mrs. Finlay," the preacher said, "have an uphill road ahead."

Phil grunted. Uphill indeed.

"I haven't walked in your shoes, so I won't give advice."

Most sensible thing he'd heard all day—

"Except to say one thing." Young preacher Gilbert, nearly as tall as Phil, placed a gentle hand on Phil's shoulder and locked gazes for a long moment. Sincerity. Patience. Trust.

Why couldn't Caroline look at him that way? Just once?

"If you and she, with that innocent babe, are to marshal through in one piece, you're going to have to dig deep, Phil. Remember every reason you fell in love with Caroline, every reason you chose her for your wife. Dust off the good memories. Embrace the good word: *Above all, love each other deeply, because love covers a multitude of sins.*"

As the sun faded to twilight on Christmas Day, Phil returned home, most uncertain of the reception awaiting him.

He rode directly to the house, swung from the saddle, and had just flipped the reins over the porch railing when Caroline came out. She wore her cloak and folded her empty arms against the wind.

But she *finally* looked at him in silent question.

He removed his hat and fought the urge to reach for her and take her into his arms. To comfort and to seek comfort.

Would they *ever* regain the satisfying closeness they'd once known?

What good was remembering what it was like to love and be loved... if he hadn't a chance to regain it? Somehow, some way, he had to patiently earn his wife's love. *Could* she love him again?

Him. Flawed. Unworthy. Broken.

The expression on her face spoke of impatience and an urgency to hear the truth.

"Mrs. Jones is dead." The mute desperation on the faces of those half-grown children— he'd *hated* himself. "Her brother and his family are there, seeing to the burying, and the children."

"And the Gilberts?"

"There. Helping." He spun his hat. The preacher had proved himself that day, earned Phil's respect. So had his young wife. What would it take for Phil to regain the Gilberts' respect?

He forced himself to meet Caroline's gaze. Almost against his will, he'd carried thoughts of Caroline close to his heart, all day. He thought he understood better now what the minister had intended in his brief sermon about remembering his love for Caroline. He had loved her, deeply.

He couldn't say when or how his love for her had waned. Maybe that gradual cooling had been the reason she'd stopped loving him in return.

"The baby?" Caroline braced herself, her arms folded snugly over her middle. Defensive. Protective.

"The brother knows of the child and the boy says she's mine. His ma didn't have anybody else around." They'd believed it too, evidenced by virulent hostility. He'd deserved their animosity. And worse.

Caroline shivered. "Do they want her?"

"Yes." Voicing the single word burned, broken glass to his raw throat.

She turned for the door, the anger he'd expected from the first *finally* erupting. She spun back, gloriously alive and animated in her fury. "They *can't* have her. You told them so, didn't you?"

He nodded. "The decision is yours, Caroline. You are my wife. You decide if the babe stays or if—" His throat constricted, cutting off words and air.

How had he been so thoughtlessly foolish, to bring his wife, his family, to this terrible crossroads? "Whatever your decision, I'll abide by it." He clenched his fists and awaited the verdict.

He *hated* himself for every stupid, selfish thought that had led him to Mrs. Jones's bedroom door. For the millionth time, he wished he'd never taken the first step away from his wife.

Caroline visibly fought to control her emotions.

He'd wanted her to shake off the funk, the numbness that had swallowed her whole since Peter's birth and death. But not like this. Never like this.

Her lower lip trembled and she folded her arms snuggly against the bitter cold. Strands of dark hair pulled free, whispering across her face in the wind. "Her name is Noelle. A Christmas baby, like my mother. She will bear my mother's name."

Caroline wanted his baby.

Relief, hot and sweet, flashed through him like a spring rainstorm.

He didn't deserve her. Either of them— not Caroline and not the baby... *Noelle.*

He took two eager steps toward her, thinking only of sweeping her into his arms, of thanking her with kisses upon her cheeks and hands.

But Caroline halted him with palms raised in warning. "I can't rest until this is settled. You go back there... to..." She closed her eyes as if forcing away images she couldn't bear. "You ensure they understand. *We* will raise *our daughter.* She is here with her brothers and sisters, and *we* are her family."

Caroline's anguished face revealed she understood precisely what she asked. The price? Noelle had a brother and sister she would never know.

"Thank you."

Caroline nodded sharply. "Go on with you. Make sure they understand."

"It's done. We agreed I'd return under one condition, if I returned the child to them. If you wanted her, I wouldn't be back."

She nodded, accepting the arrangement.

The space of several breaths passed, his showing in puffs of white. His horse tossed his head and Phil soothed the animal with strokes upon his neck.

He dreaded her response, but had to know. "Where do we go from here?"

"That depends."

He waited for her to elaborate.

Time slipped past. Evidently, she'd left it to him to discern what "depends" meant.

"I did an awful, unforgivable thing. I'm the sorriest man alive." Emotion choked him, swift and strong. A mule-kick to the gut. He squeezed his hat, his attention on the battered Stetson until he regained his composure.

Still, she didn't speak.

"I meant what I said, witnessed by the Gilberts. I beg your forgiveness. I swear to God I'll never give you cause to doubt me again." He rubbed at the ache in the vicinity of his heart, but it wouldn't let up.

Her posture softened, her shoulders slumping, just a little, but she still hadn't spoken. He didn't deserve her forgiveness, but he'd work for it, every day of his life. "Maybe, when we are old and gray, you'll come to—" *...love me again.*

The white-hot pain in his chest intensified. He would accept responsibility, beg forgiveness, but broach the subject of love? Why was that so hard to speak?

He'd never had difficulty telling his wife he loved her. *Before.*

When he'd been certain, safe in the knowledge that she loved him.

He hadn't been certain, confident, in a long while.

Now he had her attention and *must* finish. "Maybe you'll come to forgive me."

A bitter wind swirled about his legs, rattling his frozen bones. He stood in silence for several long moments more, and had nearly given up and reached for the horse's reins to lead him to the barn, when at last Caroline took a step toward him.

The porch creaked. Her boot heels dragged on the planks. And his foolish, battered heart leapt in his chest at the sight of her lopsided smile.

When had she last smiled at him? He couldn't recall.

He had no recollection of her approaching him... not since they'd lost Peter.

"Phil?" She didn't sound mad. On the contrary, she sounded like *home*.

"Yes ma'am?"

"Hurry up with your chores and get yourself inside where it's warm."

Chapter Six

On New Year's Eve, long after the older children were in bed, Caroline walked the bedroom floor with Noelle.

The sweet babe had crept into her well-guarded heart, unaware. Caroline loved her baby girl... *her* daughter. Every bit as much as she loved those she'd brought into the world.

She set the baby on the bed again, unwrapped her quickly, and assessed her daughter's belly. Distended, gaseous, bloated. Cow's milk wasn't good for her. A quick swaddling, then she snuggled Noelle to her shoulder.

A light knock on the door announced Phil. He opened it a crack. "Caroline, let me walk the floor with Noelle. You should sleep."

"Tomorrow morning, you must buy a goat. A nanny producing good milk. Noelle's stomach can't tolerate cow's milk."

"Yes ma'am." He shut the door behind him to keep the heat in, and took the baby.

As she handed off the snug, warm bundle, winter wind scraped past the house Phil had reinforced and added onto, his superior carpentry skills ensuring the home stayed warm and safe against the ravages of severe winters.

Last winter, the cabin had been claustrophobic with snowdrifts blocking the windows. Phil had been forced to tunnel through to the barn. He'd built stairs of sorts through the snow to reach the roof, where he'd shoveled off the shingles and cleared the chimneys.

That long, arduous winter had begun too early, in mid-October. With Peter's Day on February second, and spring late to arrive, that awful winter had seemed to last forever.

Through it all, this house had been her protection.

This house— *their* home— should be *all* the protection she required. She couldn't also need walls around her heart? Certainly not to protect her heart from a penitent husband.

Or did she? "How can I trust you?"

He paused, his hand on the doorknob.

Caroline's heart pounded double-time against her breastbone.

Phil turned, concern lining his face. "I promise, Caroline, tomorrow, no matter the weather, I'll find a goat. A good nanny, like you want." He searched her face, clearly aware of her hysteria. "Have I once given you cause to distrust me with our children?"

"No, no. I mean—" She gestured broadly to encompass all of it.

They'd not paused in the intervening week to talk. Instead, they'd fallen into a routine filled with the chores of living and raising little ones.

The children were small enough they'd never remember anything about how Noelle had come into their lives. Oh, to be a child, and accept newcomers to the family with ease.

One problem remained: how could Caroline forget?

Ultimately, did she *want* to?

She'd read and reread the story of Christ's birth. The verse about Mary, the mother of Jesus, returned often. *...Mary treasured up all these things and pondered them in her heart.*

She looked at Phil— really looked at him. Disheveled hair, bleary-eyed, a day's growth of dark whiskers on his chin. He'd pulled on trousers and shirt in haste. One brace held up his trousers, and the other draped alongside his leg.

He'd not paused to don his stockings.

Wasn't that a sign of a good man? He'd heard a crying babe and thought only of his wife?

Must she forget in order to forgive?

Or was it possible to treasure up memories *and* forgive?

The thick, defensive walls of ice around her heart hadn't only cracked, they'd begun to thaw in earnest.

"In an instant, I destroyed the trust built through seven years of marriage." He kissed Noelle's head as he gently jostled her. Anguish etched his features, but love was there too. Love for Noelle— a miracle in the darkness.

Caroline shivered, though the bedroom hearth was ablaze and the room warm. Phil's gaze caressed her face, lingered on her mouth, returned to her eyes. It seemed the honest, forthright man she'd fallen in love with at seventeen had returned.

Why *now*?

"It might require seven years to rebuild that trust, maybe longer. Whatever it takes, Caroline, I'm here. I'll repay that debt, one day at a time."

His sincerity knocked a great chunk of ice free from its moorings. He'd given the question of trust a good deal of thought. He wanted her trust.

"That's what you meant, isn't it?"

"Yes." Love for her husband stirred where it had lain dormant beneath winter snows.

Foolish— so foolish! How could she allow herself to *feel* for this man again? Sure, he wanted to fix things now, but what about six months from now, when she *still* couldn't feel the sunlight on her face? What if two years from now, Noelle strongly resembled Mrs. Jones?

What if her love for Phil still wasn't enough? How long would he wait? It seemed imprudent to love him... that thick, impenetrable wall had kept her safe for so long...

"Do you want to talk about it now?" He held their whimpering daughter on his shoulder with patience and security.

She shook her head.

Some questions were better left unasked because no answer would be good enough. They'd serve only to further unravel her failing marriage. She wanted to move forward, toward better times.

Very few questions and answers affected their present and future. *Those* mattered.

She'd asked one, and he'd given a satisfactory answer; trust would return, in time.

"Go ahead," he urged. "I see you have something weighty on your mind."

She fought to formulate the most distressing question of all. *Do you love me*?

This question *mattered*. The thought of the rest of their lives, barely companions, broke her heart. She needed more.

"Caroline— it's all right if you'd rather

sleep."

She shook her head, resisting the urge to climb in bed and put an end to the conversation. "Last winter, I tended sick children all night. Alone."

"I'm sorry for that night and dozens more like it. I'll make it up to you."

"*Why* are you solicitous?" She indicated the baby. "Why?"

He blinked, as if caught by surprise. "Because you loved me once. I know you did. If it takes a lifetime, I'll win your heart."

All that melting ice within her overflowed as tears, running in torrents down her cheeks.

"Caroline— I'm sorry. I don't mean to press."

"Why now?" A full year had passed without one word of assurance.

Just how long had he been in love with Mrs. Jones?

"You haven't touched me as a wife in more than a year. You avoid contact as we go about our work. *Why* would you want me to love you?"

He touched her then— his warm, big hand settling on the nape of her neck as he drew her near. His forearm rested against the long braid draped over her shoulder. He bent, to draw eye to eye. "I want you to love me, again, because you are the *one* woman I love. With all my heart."

"I want to believe you, but you never—"

He kissed her brow. The press of lips upon

her flesh sent a surge of heat from her scalp to her toes. He lingered, that single kiss silencing her argument.

He pulled away just enough to hold her gaze once more. Firelight reflected in blue. "I love you, Caroline. I've *always* loved you."

"Hold me?"

With the fussy baby in the crook of an elbow, he slipped the other arm about her. *Achingly* familiar.

Warm.

Comforting and real.

So *wonderful.*

Just as she'd asked, he held her close. He stroked her back through layers of flannel, wool, and cotton.

How did an estranged husband and wife begin anew?

A husband didn't sleep on the parlor floor for nearly a year, then suddenly make his place at his wife's side in their bed.

The time to start anew would never be perfectly right. So she held on tight to Phil, her arm about his waist. "When Noelle settles to sleep, come to bed."

He stilled.

Noelle yawned widely. She whimpered, already winding down.

"It's time you rejoined me in our bed."

Phil paced the parlor by firelight and castigated himself. *Idiot. Fool.*

Noelle gradually settled into contented sleep, and he grew more agitated.

He'd confessed love to his wife— and she'd remained silent, her expression agonized.

Of course she didn't love him in return. How could she?

Just as he'd killed the trust she had in him, he'd destroyed his wife's love. He didn't deserve her kindness, her affection...

Rebuilding trust might take seven years, a decade, more. Her love would be as elusive, if not more so.

She hadn't lied with a mumbled *I love you too*... but she'd offered a gargantuan kindness he didn't deserve.

Come to bed.

Last winter, he'd slept on the parlor floor to keep his fever to himself. So soon before her confinement with Peter, he'd tried to protect her from the illness.

Then Peter had been born, and lived mere hours. In her grief and sleeplessness, he'd not wanted to disturb what little rest she might obtain, so he'd continued to sleep in the other room.

A month or two had passed, and her condition had worsened. She lost weight, never smiled, barely shuffled from one chore to the next. Then he'd been asked to repair Widow Jones's roof...

And he'd not deserved the comfort of a bed.

Like that starving dog beneath the table, desperate for crumbs, his heart had lifted with her invitation to return. He wasn't foolish enough to confuse her offer with love.

He waited until Noelle was sound asleep before he reentered the bedroom. Caroline breathed even, deeply, the quilts tucked under her chin. Firelight danced on her long, dark braid where it had fallen from the edge of the bed.

Their bed.

Gently, he set the babe in her cradle, and tucked an additional quilt around her. Poor little mite.

Goat's milk. First thing tomorrow.

Caroline shifted beneath the bed covers. "Come to bed."

A second invitation. He wouldn't wait for a third.

As he'd done so many times before, he undressed to his Union suit and hung his clothes on the peg. He lifted the quilts, careful not to uncover her, and took his place at her side.

Falling asleep took a long while. He lay still,

savoring the comfort of the feather mattress and the nearness of the woman he loved.

He would do all he could, day after day, night after night, to rebuild, regain, and shore up their foundation. But voicing his love for her aloud? No. He'd erred, and he wouldn't make that mistake again.

Chapter Seven

By the end of January, Phil had grown quite comfortable sharing a bed with his wife. Caroline was well rested as Noelle had begun sleeping through the night almost instantly upon switching to goat's milk.

Their little family was healing, moving forward, and he couldn't be happier.

Except that today was the first of February. Tonight marked the one-year anniversary of her first labor pains to deliver Peter. She'd travailed nearly twenty hours to bring him into the world.

Far longer than with Del, Harold, Luke, Miranda, or Mary Beth. Sixth babies shouldn't take so long.

Phil had been utterly useless. Nothing could have prepared him— not assisting the Kendalls nor the Kennedys— their two closest neighbors— in calf-pulling. Not their five earlier children. He'd done the best he could to assist with Peter's birth, but the child, when finally born, had been purple, listless, and weak.

He *needed* to connect with his wife. He needed to celebrate life and love and their future. He needed to take her in his arms and let the rest of the world disappear for a long while.

Surely, in the month since she'd invited him back to their bed, she'd grown used to the idea of them resuming marital intimacies. She welcomed his kisses, hugged him often. Touched him on the shoulder as she brought platters to the table at mealtime.

Thank God in Heaven the time had finally come.

Fourteen months without his wife. Fourteen long months— other than the horrible mistake last March. Far too long to live in a state of celibacy.

But that night, after the children were asleep and they'd retired, Phil reached for his wife, held her snuggled to his side.

Love for his wife, this woman who'd given him a family, a purpose for living, filled him to bursting at the seams. They'd come so far in the past many weeks. So far.

She relaxed against him... until he kissed her.

She seemed amiable enough... until he trailed a thumb over her cheekbone.

She stiffened, pulled away, and stared at the ceiling.

"Please, Caroline." How could he ask her for intimacies? Was she recalling where he'd last been?

Ten months ago.

How many times had he offered to tell her anything about the two days he'd spent at Widow Jones's? Five? Six? Caroline insisted some questions weren't worth asking. Unless the question and answer stood in the way of them moving forward, toward better times, she didn't want to know.

Apparently, he and his wife didn't see eye to eye on the matter.

She might say she's forgiving him, might believe it in her heart. But when it came right down to living as man and wife, the truth presented itself in all its ugliness.

Why had he followed the pastor's instructions to recall why he loved his wife? If he hadn't resurrected his love for Caroline, he wouldn't be alone in his marriage, loving a woman who couldn't love him in return.

How long would she punish him?

February second, the first anniversary of Peter's Day, dawned cold and blustery, but the sun was shining and by noon, the wind had quieted and the day promised to be mild.

Perfect conditions for a brief stop at the cemetery. Caroline hadn't been to Peter's graveside since last spring, hoping staying away would help her heal. Today would be a good time to return.

"Hitch up the sleigh, will you?" Caroline asked of her husband. "I'll ready the children. We're going to town."

"Why?" His dark brows drew together in confusion.

"Have you honestly forgotten the significance of this day?" How could he *possibly* have forgotten Peter existed— was this like *"forgetting"* his marital vows?

"You didn't want to take them to church on Sunday— why are we going to town today?"

"How could you have forgotten what today is?'"

"I've forgotten nothing." His voice, usually warm and filled with affection had turned hard. In his eyes, she saw resentment, no doubt over last night and her inability to forget.

He'd wanted loving, while her heart and mind groaned under the weight of memories. That long, long labor had worn her threadbare and exhausted Peter. He'd not been strong enough to fight.

How could she lose herself in loving her husband with memories like those weighing her down?

"Our son," he emphasized, "is not in that cemetery. We're as close to him here, in our home, as anywhere. Why risk the health of many small children, to sit by a cold stone marker?"

"Marker?" Last she'd known, Peter's grave was identified only by a wooden cross she'd lashed together and stuck into the soil.

"Yes. I had a gravestone made."

"You didn't think to tell me?"

"*When,* Caroline? When would I have told you?" Vexed, he propped both fists on lean hips, and towered over her. "While you stared into the fire and ignored my presence? When we climbed in bed together one *summer* evening?"

Anger had turned his voice ugly, harsh. He was right, of course.

"Do you know, last March and April, combined, you and I had one conversation? *One.* And it hurt as bad as pulling an infected molar."

"I wasn't well." The justification sounded weak, paltry, insufficient. "I wasn't myself."

"No, Mrs. Finlay, and you're still not well.

You're not yourself. You're not the girl I married."

He didn't wait for a response. Without pausing for his coat, threw open the door and slammed it behind himself.

Only then did emotion eek through cracks in the frozen surface of her soul. *Disappointment.*

Her husband was furious, angry, and all she could muster was mild disappointment.

A full year—

Would she *never* be well?

Caroline had barely rolled the laundry tub into the kitchen and begun heating water on the stove when Phil burst back inside.

He breathed heavily, as if he'd been running. His skin was damp with perspiration and a bit of straw stuck to his shirt front and clung to his hair. She suspected he'd been mucking out stalls.

He slammed the door against the cold air, and in two long strides, swept her into his arms.

"Phillip!"

He kissed her. Hard. With passion and... *love*, much like he had when they'd been newlyweds. His kisses awakened her in a way little else could.

He spun her around, then set her on her toes. Dizzy, she gripped his vest. "What's got into you?"

"I'm in love with my wife, and I won't remain quiet about it any longer. I love you, Caroline, and if you want to go to town, we'll go to town."

"You love me?"

"Woman!" he kissed her once more, hard, then another that lingered. "I love you. You don't have to say you love me back."

"But I do."

His smile carried gallons of sunshine. "I know."

"You know? How do you know?"

He shook his head, brushing aside her question. "We've been granted a second chance, Mrs. Finlay, and I refuse to let it pass us by. Seems to me we have two options. We can mope and suffer and barely get along, or we can seize this life we live by both horns and love each other with everything we've got."

Pain itched behind her breastbone. "But I'm not the girl you married."

"No. Forgive me, Caroline. That was a mean, fool thing to say. I take it back."

"Apology accepted."

"You're not the girl I married," he began again, soft and sincere. "You're better. Stronger, more experienced, infinitely more beautiful. You're the mother of my children."

Somehow, in there, she knew he included Noelle. Yes, she was Noelle's mother. Completely.

"We missed Christmas," he announced.

"We were rather busy." Noelle had arrived on Christmas Eve. He'd spent Christmas Day at the Joneses.

"What do you say to rewinding the clock and making today Christmas Eve?"

Grief scoured her heart raw. "It's the second of February."

"The children don't know any different."

His warm hold on her waist anchored her, reminded her of how far they'd come.

"You could bake the gingerbread men I love so much. I'll bring in the perfect evergreen tree. We'll sing carols and wind garlands over the porch railing. I think it's just the thing we need to make it through."

Perhaps he was right. So far, they'd grieved, each in their own way, and they'd not been successful. Left to herself, she'd slipped back into that dangerous downhill slope into despair.

Thank goodness this strong, capable man worked beside her, keeping her grounded and secure. With Phil at her side, she was infinitely stronger than alone.

Together, they had every chance of succeeding. "Yes."

"Yes?" Hope lit his handsome eyes.

"Yes. The children will be thrilled."

"I have just the thing." Phil clapped his hands, rubbed them together, then nudged her aside. He rolled up his shirtsleeves then poured steaming water into the wash tub.

He sliced strips of soap into the water.

"What are you doing?" She couldn't help but laugh. Him, preparing to wash clothes? She'd never seen the like!

"Am I doing this wrong? It's my first try, you know."

"I do know."

"I've watched you, Mrs. Finlay, and I've come to the conclusion that gifts of service are my best chance of winning your heart."

"Oh, Phil." She leaned against his back, looped her arms about his middle and nestled her cheek against his back. "You've won my heart already. It's yours."

"That was this morning. I'd best ensure your heart is mine this afternoon."

"I'm not so easily swayed, am I?"

"No, my dearest wife. You are steadfast and immovable, and for that, I'm grateful."

Tears filled her eyes. But this time, they were tears of happiness. She didn't want to cry, but she wanted to retain the ability to— just in case a good reason presented itself.

"Let's get the laundry done and hung to dry. I can't wait to pull the oldest three out on a sled to find a Christmas tree."

Chapter Eight

"Happy Anniversary, Wife."

Caroline glanced up from the batter she whipped with a wooden spoon. The depth and timbre of his voice still evoked tingles within her, after seven mostly happy years together.

"Merry Christmas." She smiled, easily. Her heart felt light and at ease for the first time in nearly a year. She rather liked his suggestion that they turn back time and enjoy Christmas together.

He must've been encouraged by her smile,

because he drew near and rested his hands on her shoulders. At her back, his presence felt so solid, certain, warm. She paused in her meal preparations to simply savor his touch.

Now that the sun had begun to shed warming, soothing light in the dark recesses of her heart and mind once more, she could see how bleak the past months had been. She'd been going through the motions, living... but not living.

Odd, how such a shocking surprise could bring about healing. Not unlike cauterizing a flesh wound with burning metal— it hurt, but it saved and salvaged and repaired.

She leaned back into her husband's strength, enjoying the precious moment.

The kitchen smelled wonderful— roasting ham, creamed potatoes, yeasty dinner rolls. High notes of cinnamon and ginger graced the air in the gingerbread cookies Phil so loved.

"The children are napping." He nuzzled her neck. "Put me to work. What can I do to help?"

Another fine example of his daily— no, hourly— efforts to win her love. And win her, he had. Love for this good-hearted man had returned in full measure. She doubted she'd ever stopped loving him. But in her grief, she'd forgotten to reach out to him, to stand with him against the storms and challenges of life.

Mistakes she had no intention of repeating. "Hold me for a minute?"

The weight of his hands tightened, then he hugged her about the waist. "Always. Whatever you need, whatever you want, I'm here."

If only he'd said those words on the day they'd lost Peter. How they might have made a difference.

A twinge of responsibility whispered through her soul. She hadn't said those words to him, either, and that realization shamed her. He'd lost their son, too. Forever the stronger, he'd built a box, and dug the grave. He'd held her while she cried.

She hadn't held *him*.

Regret mingled with the sweet recognition that he'd suffered alongside her, in his own way, bereft, in need, just like she'd been. Why hadn't she reached out to him?

Now, in full light of day, she saw how much her dear husband needed a simple touch to feel loved. A squeeze to his shoulder. Her hand within his as they prayed. The brush of her fingertips at his back when he kissed her good morning. Words mattered to him too, but without touch, words didn't bear much weight. Not to Phil.

It wasn't too late to hold him.

Dropping the wooden spoon into the batter bowl, Caroline turned in her husband's arms and hugged him tight.

Had she ever really hugged *him*? Or had he always held her?

He returned her desperate embrace, and in the cocooned warmth and safety of this hug, she remembered falling in love with him, recalled numerous reasons she loved him still.

This man held her heart and always would. She knew what she wanted, what she needed from the days, weeks, and years ahead. She knew what she wanted their future to be like.

"Phil?" Her voice sounded so small in the snug space against his chest. As if they were entirely alone in the world.

His caress at the nape of her neck felt so good, easing the tightness in her muscles.

"Hmmm?" He eased back just enough to tuck a knuckle beneath her chin and urge her to look at him. His eyes had never seemed so blue. Deep, rich, dark... and filled with love so exquisite, she couldn't doubt he loved her still.

"Today marks seven years walking side by side." His caress along her jaw raised tingles of awareness in their wake, reminding her she felt so alive, as if all color had returned to her world.

His gaze clouded. "God willing, we have many more ahead. I want to take that journey with you." He brushed a feather-light kiss across her lips. "I want to hold your hand every day of my life." Another kiss, this one lingered and sealed the promise. "I want to continue building a family with you—" He rested his forehead against hers. "I'll pray the good Lord forgives me, and one day, you might, too."

She nodded, as her throat had closed.

"I'm sorry, Caroline. Sorrier than I know how to say." His thumb brushed away a trail of tears from her cheek. He pressed a kiss to that wetness.

These weren't tears of anger, grief, nor humiliation... happy tears this time. But emotion welled so hot and heavy in her chest and throat.

"I've no right to expect you to forgive me, not for a good, long while, but I have to ask. Please. Forgive me." His voice, strangled and sincere, conveyed the honesty of his plea. Not new words, of course. He'd begged her understanding and forgiveness.

But this time was different.

Perhaps because *she* was different.

And today was special, a day for miracles and healing and forgiveness. If she couldn't forgive her husband, and herself, at this holy time of year, when the gift of a baby brought light into a dark world, when *could* she?

The words still couldn't push past the lump in her throat, so she reached up and kissed her husband. A kiss filled with tenderness, love, and passion. A kiss unlike any they'd shared in far too long. A kiss to signal a new beginning, a new page in the storybook of their lives.

He responded with fire and urgency and desperation. Gradually, their kisses softened, until tenderness and awe and love overflowed.

"I love you, Phil." She swallowed, fighting

the fist-sized lump in her throat. "And I'm sorry. I apologize."

His embrace tightened. With her ear to his chest, she heard the steady beating of his heart. "You haven't a thing to apologize for." He pressed a kiss to her temple. "And I *love you*, Caroline, more than I ever thought possible. More than the day we wed."

The steady beat of his heart; quick, lively, so full of life and vitality. She had far more to be grateful for this Christmas than she'd previously realized. "Thank you."

"I'm indebted to you, not the other way 'round."

She chuckled. "Not the way I see it."

"Oh?"

"Thank you for coming back to me." He could've chosen differently. The thought made her heart ache.

"I never left." A tear slipped from his chin and into her hair. "God, I'm sorry..."

"I love you, Phil. I always have. Still do. You're my husband... the forgiving is done."

He stilled. Another tear slipped from his jaw and down her cheek, but rather than dashing them away on his shirtsleeve like she expected he'd do, he clung tighter.

A long moment passed as she clung to her husband, relished his heat, his nearness, this embrace that healed far more than their battered hearts.

"Thank you," he whispered. "I don't deserve you, your mothering kindness to Noelle— and I certainly don't deserve your love."

That kind of talk must stop. "Listen." She pushed back and sought his gaze. "Like I told you on Christmas Day night, on the front porch. Noelle is *mine*." That hadn't come out right. She shook her head, started over. "That precious baby girl is *ours*. No more talk, *none*— you understand?— no more talk of 'my' daughter. She's ours. Just like Miranda and Mary Beth. *Our daughter*."

"How is this possible?" He cupped her face in that gentle way of his, just like he had the day he'd first declared himself, on a summer's day, so long ago.

At moments like this, life seemed simple. Easy. Perfect.

She saw everything clearly.

"Maybe it's our own Christmas miracle. Noelle filled the void in my heart left by Peter. I thought that wound would never heal—but *she* healed me. And you gave her to me."

He shook his head, awestruck. So endearing she couldn't help but chuckle.

She initiated another kiss, this one sweet and pure. Tears stung her eyes.

"*You* are the miracle." His warm breath tickled her ear.

Winter wind blasted frost against the snug little house, but not a single draft disturbed their peace. The children slept on, probably would for a while yet. She knew just the thing to ensure their happily-ever-after began on the right foot.

Entwining her fingers with his, she led him to their bedroom door and pulled him inside. It took a mere moment to communicate her intention by slipping one button free on his shirt front, then two.

Happiness lit his handsome features by light of the fire in the hearth. His kiss ignited a fire deep within her belly and deft fingers worked her buttons free. He broke away long enough to grab his shirt at the back of his neck and pull it off. Woolen underwear came next.

She chuckled as he shucked the rest of their clothes and led her to their marriage bed.

Phil dozed, his arm about his wife's slim waist... until she sat upright in one panicked move. "I forgot the photographer."

She pulled free, swung her legs over the edge of the bed, and reached for her chemise. "I can't believe I forgot."

"I took care of it."

She let her shift float into place over her body. Backed by firelight, she'd never been more beautiful. "You did?"

"Of course. It's tradition." They'd had a wedding portrait made on their first Christmas together. Baby Del had come along by their second Christmas, and another portrait, expensive though they were, was all either one of them had needed or wanted. This Christmas could not be the first year they interrupted that tradition. Delayed or not, this Christmas was too important.

"He'll be here at three o'clock. We have time." He reached for her hand, inviting her to return to the warmth and seclusion of their bed.

Struck again by his good fortune, by the miracles gracing his family, he simply had to be the luckiest man alive. Had he ever been more in love?

"I propose a new tradition." Phil nuzzled his wife's nape.

To his delight, she snuggled back against him, bringing to mind the intimacies and joy they'd found together just that morning. With the photographer's business completed and the children fed and back down for an afternoon nap, it seemed the right time to present his wife with a Christmas gift he hoped she'd cherish.

"Oh?"

Her touch upon his cheek ignited his blood. "Yes. A new beginning deserves a new tradition."

"I like the sound of that."

"I think it'll serve us well on every Christmas to come as the children grow."

"What is this new tradition?" She rested her hands over his, snug about her middle. She felt so good, flush against him, smelled so good, too. Like soap and flowery toilet water, and in her finest dress. The best she'd worn for a long while. He loved her more than ever.

"Come. I'll show you." He seated her beside him on the settee in the parlor and offered the stocking he'd hung on the mantel. Paper rustled within as he handed it to her.

"We already enjoyed the orange and nuts from St. Nick."

"Reach inside."

She pulled out his note and unfolded it. Tipping it toward the waning daylight streaming through the windowpanes, she read his words. He'd tried to get it right, tried to express everything in his heart, as his soul yearned to reconnect with her— for good this time. He wanted this note to last, to be a memoir she'd keep, return to when she desired to recapture the magic of this special day and their new beginning.

He watched her face as she read, tucked an

arm about her shoulders as she pressed her lips together with a swell of emotion.

She finished reading and blotted her eyelids with trembling fingertips. "Thank you. I'll keep this always."

He smiled, more at peace than he'd been in years. more in love than he'd been in years. "Let's do this each Christmas. Include the little ones as they grow. Notes of reassurance, love, I.O.U.s for gifts of time and cooperative work. I picture a note in Del's stocking, good for a pony of his choosing."

She chuckled and rested her head on his shoulder. "I see this parlor filled with family. Down the road, we'll have to add on to this house. Expand this room, add bedrooms. A staircase with rooms above." He gestured with an extended arm, mapping the additions he'd build as the years marched on. "Years from now, we'll sit here and open stockings just like this one, with notes from everyone, to each beloved family member."

"I like the idea, very much."

"Is it one you can stick with, every Christmas Day for the rest of our lives?"

She pretended to think it over, and he had to chuckle. He couldn't help it.

"With you," she whispered, tugging on his heart, "I'm up for anything."

Chapter Nine

Epilogue

December 24, 1890
Nine years later...

Some traditions, Caroline Finlay determined, were easier carried out than others.

Through the years, their family had nearly doubled in size. Convincing their brood of active children, the youngest not quite two, to sit still and read notes their brothers and sisters had written had proved more a circus than a cherished experience.

Caroline noticed Phil's growing impatience.

The oldest boys, Del and Harold, now aged fifteen and fourteen, thought the exercise in family love absurd and wouldn't read any of their Christmas notes aloud. The little ones, who'd worked so diligently to write legibly, to share meaningful thoughts with their eldest brothers, ended up in tears.

An hour into the exercise, both Jeanette, not quite two, and Ivy Mae, age six, were in tears. Timothy and Dallas, at seven and four, had taken to wrestling each other and yelling.

Mary Beth must have sneaked a book to read because she was quite settled in her own world.

Noelle, nine years of age, promised to be a great beauty. She resembled her father, sisters, brothers, and much to Caroline's joy— the whole community of Mountain Home insisted she looked just like Caroline. But that beautiful child had pulled a mean face, scowling at her brothers, one of whom must've thrown a spit-wad because the evidence dangled from her dark curls.

Caroline took her husband's hand and squeezed. She tried her best not to chuckle. "Let's call a recess, shall we?"

"I'd rather call it quits."

"That seems like a wise idea."

"Hooray!" Luke, at thirteen, had grown a full foot— or at least it seemed so— in the past month alone. He picked up Dallas, tickled him without mercy, and carried the laughing child up the staircase. His boots pounded on the treads, echoing in the stairwell and adding to the cacophony.

"Miranda, Mary Beth," Caroline caught both daughters by the elbows as they attempted to escape. "It's your turn to care for the little ones. Please put the youngest four down for a nap."

"A nap?" Miranda rolled her eyes. "Mother, Timothy is seven. He doesn't need a nap."

"Any growing boy with enough energy to harass his siblings needs a nap. You tell him I said so."

"Quiet time!" Phil bellowed up the stairs at the retreating children. "One hour. No one comes out of their rooms."

"But, Papa!" Ivy Mae stood by the front door, somehow already in her coat, scarf, hat, and mittens. "I play in the snow!"

Phil scooped up the little girl and squeezed her in a hug. "After you've had a quiet hour. You need to rest."

"No! I don't need rest. I need to play."

"Mama and Papa need a nap. So do you."

Ivy Mae cried all the while as she peeled off her winter clothing and dragged her limp self up the stairs.

Once all the children were in their rooms, doors closed but far from settled down, Caroline shut her husband and herself into their bedroom on the main floor.

"That's it. No more Christmas stocking tradition for this family." Phil sat on the edge of the bed and unlaced his boots. He lay back and covered his eyes with a forearm. "Let Santa bring raisins and nuts and oranges next year. I never should have suggested the foolish idea in the first place."

Caroline sat on the bed and laid one knitted stocking— Phil's— on his chest. "This year, husband, stockings are just for us. I think the idea may need to grow on some of our children."

Phil sat up, and squeezing the gray stocking, made the papers crinkle. "I liked seeing the older children give acts of kindness to the little ones. Sometimes it works."

"That's right. And that's why we're not reverting to fruit and nuts in stockings. No peppermint sticks for us."

"Why not?"

"Because I have a vision in mind, Mr. Finlay. As I recall, you told me our home would expand. It's time for you to build onto this house again. We need a larger parlor and a dining room twice the size of what we have."

"You peeked at the love letter I put in your stocking."

"I did not." But she smiled. She couldn't

wait to read his letter, to savor every word, and to tuck it away in the cedar chest he'd built for her as a wedding gift. She'd saved many precious things in that chest, but Phil's notes were among the most treasured. "But I will."

He reached for her hand. She lay beside him on the bed, snuggling her head on his shoulder. "Our children will grow up. They'll understand the importance of Christmas eventually."

"Ha. I'll believe that when I see it."

"They'll understand, because we'll teach them."

"Why are you so patient?" he asked. "How can you love naughty boys?"

That made her smile. *Ah, Phil.* A dear man who couldn't quite understand that a mother's love— and a wife's love— were bottomless.

"You're not angry?" he asked.

"Not at all. They're children."

"What about me?"

She pushed up on one elbow, to better see his face. Stark vulnerability, the like of which she'd not seen since the year of Noelle's birth, dimmed her husband's blue eyes. She'd have to help him banish that nonsense.

Love worked miracles. She knew that truth, through and through. She'd love Phil Finlay until vulnerability, hopelessness, and self-doubts couldn't take root.

She spread her hand over her husband's

heart and waited until he met her gaze. "I'm not angry with you, Phil. I love you. I believe I've always loved you."

"I found two gray hairs this week while shaving. I'm getting old."

"I'll love you when you're fully gray, and even if you're bald."

"You will?"

"Absolutely."

"Why?"

Men could be incredibly dense, especially her man. If she could give her husband any gift at all, she'd erase that insecurity from his very soul. But that might change his nature, and she couldn't have that. She loved Phil Finlay exactly as he was.

"Because, my dear husband, my love for you does not depend upon the color or quantity of hairs upon your head. I loved you when I was seventeen, and I'll love you when I'm ninety-and-seven."

"Why?"

If he weren't so earnest, so desperate for answers, she'd brush aside the repetitive question, argue he sounded like a three-year-old, forever asking *why*. But he was in earnest. And he needed to know.

"Because you've walked beside me these past sixteen years. We've faced life's challenges, hand in hand, side by side. Together, we're raising a family that has expanded my ability to love by twenty-fold."

"We only have eleven children." Good. He'd counted Peter *and* Noelle.

"All right. Together, we're raising a family that has expanded my ability to love by eleven-fold. Even if it doesn't sound as impressive."

"Go on. You were telling me why you love me."

She chuckled, loving his smile. Even more, loving the way he looked at her as if she were still, after all this time, the center of his universe.

"I love you because when I'm with you, my heart is lighter, my joy fuller, and my ability to turn my face toward sunlight is complete. With you, I grieve on February second because I remember a child we created, loved, and lost. I wouldn't trade that anniversary for the world."

"You wouldn't?"

"No, I wouldn't." Phil truly was dense when it came to matters of the heart. "If I hadn't loved you, Peter wouldn't have been born. If I hadn't loved you, I wouldn't have climbed out the other side of that life-altering experience. Without you, dear husband, my life would've been rather dull."

Regret dampened the twinkle in his eye, and she knew he remembered *The Incident.* "The Hard Winter" of '80 to '81 and the circumstances of Noelle's birth the following Christmas Eve.

Likely, he'd always feel twinges of regret when he remembered, not unlike memories of Peter, that still brought sadness. Perhaps that was the way life worked. Yet those moments of sadness were overshadowed by the happiness they'd built together.

"Without you, Phil, I wouldn't be a mother. I wouldn't have a house bursting at the seams with children."

He opened his mouth to speak— probably to apologize— so she pressed her forefinger over his lips to silence him.

"Shh. It's my turn to talk."

He chuckled and kissed her fingertip.

"You promised me your heart, Phil Finlay, and I do believe you've made good on that promise."

His smile slowly faded, seriousness reclaiming his handsome, lean features. "I love you, Mrs. Finlay, significantly more than I did the Christmas Day we wed. Do you know that?"

"I do, indeed."

"Do you love me?"

Though he'd asked the question far too often through the years, she'd never tire of promising him her love was secure, vowing she'd love him every day of her life.

So, that Christmas Eve, as befitted their sixteenth wedding anniversary and ten napping children, she swore yet again that her love was true.

And when the children revolted against the "Quiet Hour" edict precisely sixty minutes after their banishment to the second story, and found

Papa and Mama's bedroom door locked, Caroline giggled as if she were still eighteen. She pressed her mouth into her husband's shoulder and laughed with all the joy and love bubbling within her.

Somehow, through all the ups and downs, the happiness far surpassed the dark times.

Through it all, Phil remained the one constant, the greatest of her blessings.

The End

Please *share* this book with a friend
Paperbacks are easy to loan.

Please *recommend* this book.
Please share your thoughts on this book with friends.

Please post a *review*.
Reviews from readers make all the difference to those browsing and buying, as well as to writers. Please take a moment and leave an honest review— a few words will do.

One Quick Link.
to easily leave a review anywhere this book is sold (plus Goodreads):

www.kristinholt.com/one-quick-click-this-noelle

OR, shorter (pay attention to capitals and lower case):
https://bit.ly/2zDub9u

HOLIDAYS IN MOUNTAIN HOME
Series

as of September 2018
(with many more titles to follow):
In Chronological Order:

Courting Miss Cartwright (Rocky & Felicity),
1879
Book #5, Founder's Day NOVELLA

This Noelle (Phil & Caroline), **1881**
Prequel: Book #0.5, Christmas NOVELLA

The Gunsmith's Bride (Morgan & Elizabeth),
1885
Book #6, Independence Day NOVELLA

Unmistakably Yours (Hank & Jane, Oscar &
Ina), **1887**
Book #8, Thanksgiving NOVEL

Home for Christmas (Hunter & Miranda), **1898**
Book #1, Christmas NOVELLA

Maybe This Christmas (Luke & Effie), **1899**
Book #2, <u>Christmas</u> NOVELLA

The Witching Eve (Gus & Noelle), **1900**
Title #7, <u>Halloween</u> SHORT STORY

The Marshal's Surrender (Gus & Noelle), **1900**
Book #3, <u>Christmas</u> NOVEL

The Drifter's Proposal (Malloy & Adaline), **1900**
Book #4, <u>Christmas</u> NOVELLA

Find links to website pages dedicated to each book on the Holidays in Mountain Home Series Page:
www.KristinHolt.com/holidays-in-mountain-home-series

(case is irrelevant, but it's critical to spell Kristin with two i's and no e's; "Kristin is e-free")

𝓑𝓸𝓸𝓴𝓼 𝓫𝔂 𝓚𝓻𝓲𝓼𝓽𝓲𝓷 𝓗𝓸𝓵𝓽

www.KristinHolt.com

Be the first to hear about new releases, sales, and subscriber-only extras by subscribing to my monthly newsletter.

Learn more about Kristin Holt's Series:

THE HUSBAND-MAKER TRILOGY

PROSPERITY'S MAIL ORDER BRIDES

SIX BRIDES FOR SIX GIDEONS

HOLIDAYS IN MOUNTAIN HOME

~ And **collaborative works** ~

About the Author

KRISTIN HOLT

Sweet Romance
Victorian American West

Hi! I'm Kristin Holt, *USA Today* bestselling author of Sweet Romances (G- and PG-rated) set in the Victorian American West.

www.KristinHolt.com

While secular in nature, my titles are "Appropriate for All Audiences" and appeal to selective readers and fans of Inspirational and Christian historical romance.

I love to hear from readers! Please drop me a note: email me at *Kristin@KristinHolt.com.*

I write frequent articles about the **nineteenth century American west– every subject of possible interest to readers**, amateur historians, authors... as all of these tidbits surfaced while researching for my books.

http://bit.ly/2aiinNC
(case sensitive)

Or find me on Facebook. Here's my FB Profile Page:

http://bit.ly/2axfURD
(case sensitive)

And my Facebook Author Fan Page: *Kristin Holt, Sweet Victorian Western Romance*

http://bit.ly/2avSBG3
(case sensitive)

You're invited to join a fantastic Facebook group for authors and readers of Western Historical Romances, **Pioneer Hearts**.

www.facebook.com/groups/pioneerhearts

or, more simply:

http://bit.ly/1ElS5S8

(case sensitive)

As of Autumn 2018, Pioneer Hears has almost 5,000 Readers and 409 Authors. We talk Western Historical Romance, give away prizes, share books we've loved, announce new releases, and connect as friends.

#PioneerHearts

Please stop by www.KristinHolt.com and say hello!

Kristin

www.ingramcontent.com/pod-product-compliance
Lightning Source LLC
Chambersburg PA
CBHW030556130626
46552CB00006B/2565